Dear Parents and Educators,

Welcome to Penguin Young Readers! A̶.̶.̶.̶
know that each child develops at their ̶o̶.̶.̶.̶
critical thinking, and, of course, reading. ̶.̶.̶.̶
recognizes this fact. As a result, each Penguin Young Readers book
is assigned a traditional easy-to-read level (1–4) as well as an
F&P Text Level (A–P). Both of these systems will help you choose the
right book for your child. Please refer to the back of each book
for specific leveling information. Penguin Young Readers features
esteemed authors and illustrators, stories about favorite characters,
fascinating nonfiction, and more!

Who Ate My Book?

LEVEL **2**

F&P TEXT
LEVEL **E**

This book is perfect for a **Progressing Reader** who:
- can figure out unknown words by using picture and context clues;
- can recognize beginning, middle, and ending sounds;
- can make and confirm predictions about what will happen in the text; and
- can distinguish between fiction and nonfiction.

Here are some **activities** you can do during and after reading this book:
- Rhyming Words: On a separate piece of paper, make a list of all the
  rhyming words in this story. For example, *goat* rhymes with *coat*, so
  write those two words next to each other.
- Sight Words: Sight words are frequently used words that readers must
  know just by looking at them. They are known instantly, on sight. Knowing
  these words helps children develop into efficient readers. As you read the
  story, have the child point out the sight words below.

big	down	look	run	were
can	jump	me	see	you

Remember, sharing the love of reading with a child is the best gift
you can give!

*This book has been officially leveled by using the F&P Text Level Gradient™ leveling system.

In memory of Harry,
who would never, ever have
eaten your book—TK

PENGUIN YOUNG READERS
An Imprint of Penguin Random House LLC, New York

Penguin supports copyright. Copyright fuels creativity, encourages diverse voices,
promotes free speech, and creates a vibrant culture. Thank you for buying an authorized edition
of this book and for complying with copyright laws by not reproducing, scanning, or distributing any
part of it in any form without permission. You are supporting writers and allowing Penguin to
continue to publish books for every reader.

Copyright © 2020 by Tina Kügler. All rights reserved. Published by Penguin Young Readers,
an imprint of Penguin Random House LLC, New York. Manufactured in China.

Visit us online at www.penguinrandomhouse.com.

Library of Congress Cataloging-in-Publication Data is available upon request.

ISBN 9780593094709 (pbk)   10 9 8 7 6 5 4 3 2 1
ISBN 9780593094693 (hc)   10 9 8 7 6 5 4 3 2 1

PENGUIN YOUNG READERS

LEVEL
PROGRESSING
READER
2

WHO ATE MY BOOK?

by Tina Kügler

My Goat

My pet is a goat.

Hello, goat.

My goat ate his oats.

My goat ate my boat.

My goat ate my coat.

Do you want a pet goat?

My goat can run.

My goat can kick.

My goat can jump.

No, no, goat!

11

My Fish

My pet is a fish.

Hello, fish.

I look at my fish.

My fish looks at me.

My fish swims up.

My fish swims down.

My fish swims all day.

I wish I were a fish.

Look, I see a goat.

Hello, goat.

19

The goat ate my plate.

The goat ate my skate.

No, no, goat!

My Dog

My pet is a dog.

Hello, dog.

My dog can dig.

My dog can roll.

My dog is big.

My dog is warm.

My dog loves me.

Good dog.

Look, I see a goat.

Hello, goat.

The goat ate my pail.

The goat ate my mail.

No, no, goat!

Look, look!

The goat ate this book!

CHOMP!